Advance Praise for *SAM:*

"Habiger's spare and moving poem illuminates that wordless experience we humans endlessly try to explain: the act of being in love."

   - Ina Russell, editor of Jeb and Dash, A Diary of Gay Love,
1918-1945

"J.N. Habiger's *SAM: A Mundane Love Affair Between Two Men*, from the up and coming new press 11:11, is as much a love affair between two human beings as it is a love affair of language. Reminiscent of the clear and provocative poetry of Richard Brautigan, *SAM* leaps across the page and explores the world of a love affair and language in its dreamy, nearly imagistic visions of, say, an 'Attic of stars tiptoeing through his head,' so that when we reach a passage like, 'They had then/realized that/something more/was/being said,' we know this to be true of the poetry as well. And so we travel through the mindscape of memory and imagination snaking down the page, as 'words/with meaning lost/ their light…' and learn 'to understand/a certain sort/of language.' And we come to know that through poetry, 'wind/makes/music/ through/these/branches.' And like the poetic language struggling to lift us out of the 'Mundane,' so are the lovers in *SAM* 'Men/of resentment/in this world/of things.' Transcendence in love, transcendence in language, ultimately, as the epigraph from Camus suggests, leads us to 'allow/the day/to simply/happen.' And love of another, love of language means 'The city hasn't/ made me hard.' To love, to write, to create 'a line with a word,' and the 'hopeful isolation/of a message/being sent,' these are the rebellions that make the mundane sacred."

   - Douglas Cole, author of Bali Poems and Western Dream

"*SAM: A Mundane Love Affair Between Two Men* lives outside of time and space, in universes made from single rooms, or streets that materialize for the sake of their being there. Habiger has managed to write something that is both distant and intimate, fragile yet consistent."

   - Mike Corrao, author of Man, Oh Man!

SAM:

A Mundane Love Affair
Between Two Men

J. N. Habiger

ELEVEN
II:II
ELEVEN
PRESS

SAM: A MUNDANE LOVE AFFAIR BETWEEN TWO MEN

Library of Congress: 201-89-34519
ISBNs: 978-1-948687-00-3 (paperback), 978-1-948687-01-0 (ebook)

:N:

FIRST AMERICAN EDITION

Printed in the United States of America
9 8 7 6 5 4 3 2 1

In instances
where art does
not imitate life,
it's support and
encouragement
that make the
difference.

I love you,
Jeffery

TABLE OF CONTENTS

CHAPTER 1 | 2

Shadows into Sparrows

&

Moments before the Moon

CHAPTER 2 | 50

Sparrows into Owls
&
The World of Things

CHAPTER 3 | 108

Owls into Ghosts
&
Within the Distant City

CHAPTER 4 | 168

Ghosts into Children
&
An Empire of Thought

CHAPTER 5 | 222

Children into Lovers

&

The World Within the Other

"The only way to deal with an unfree world is to become so absolutely free that your very existence is an act of rebellion."

Albert Camus

Shadows into Sparrows
&
Moments before the Moon

001

Behind the clouds,

in the moments
before
the
moon,

wraith-like

shadows

raced along
the
ground.

"Why do you always?"

A voice murmured

as he walked

up the road.

The

sun

was

perched

upon

the

trees.

And he

was

without

the

danger

of tears.

"What will they
be saying next..."

He asked

himself scarcely

ruffling
the serenity

of his
expression.

He knew that this

would always

be the

same.

002

Grey tongued

and tucked

in his head

in the most

uncanny manner.

His thoughts

rattled madly

with the
wind.

The attic

of

stars

still

tip-toeing
through
his
head.

"How could they sleep?"

He shivered to himself.

"It's a privilege!"

They
        scolded
                savagely.

His innocent eyes
too narrow
to remember
        the question
                now.

"He's become a monster..."

Whispered
in the sigh
of wide wooden
floorboards.

003

There was

a howl

in his ear

with the cold

against his feet

and his

black dog

backed into

a corner.

In spite of the
protection,
the mirror
made
a horrible face.

And suddenly
he remembered.

004

Isolated

on a back road,

he would

often talk

to a tramp

and

a thief with

a sugary smile.

He would make

his way through

the shadows.

And he

often thought

of main street.

And

the

                    people
        under

            the

    lights.

            And

    how

            their

    shadows
    seemed to
    intermingle.

005

He would
      occasionally
          be
        perfectly
      content.

      The words
          would
          worsen
              then
              from
        murmurs to howls.

        And he would stand
            still,

      and

   listen.

      At times

  they

    then

         subsided.

13

And

he

remembered

the

times

he

screamed.

And

screamed.

006

A light was

    already on

   when they

      made him

     small

     and

   vulnerable.

"I've been waiting."

    He heard
      Muffled
         in a rasp.

"Why didn't you come?"

They questioned
as though speaking
through
their
teeth.

It was
because
people
were
often
frightened
of him
that
he
didn't
go
out.

He

couldn't

bare

their

whispers.

007

He was

      tongue tied,

        and an

        electric

           voice was

    calling.

        Sam seemed
        to know
        his name
        well
        enough
        to
        say
            hello.

Looking up
at Sam without
      the faintest
appropriate
expression.

    He smiled.

"Hello."

It was

seldom

that he

spoke

when

anybody

was

around.

Though
his look assured him.

Sam understood.

They had then
realized that
something more
was
being said.

008

Yellow

chrysanthemums
reminded him
of Sam.

When from
off the window,
they reflected
into the sky
a glowing
radiance.

The sun was

of

spectacular

plainness.

And
the
thought
of Sam
became
a
familiar
comfort.

009

He tried to pretend
    to be
        like
            the others.

But it wasn't seeming to help much.

    He often trailed off
                    in

distraction.

    But Sam
    still knew
    what he was
    saying.

Sam was more

straightforward

than he was.

    And handsome.

And somehow
    he could always
        interpret his silences.

010

A fresh gust of wind

took his mind

away for a

moment.

"Sam's glance is
often just as soft."

He thought

to himself

nervously.

And suddenly
the rain began,
briskly returning
his focus.

"Now don't you..."

A voice emerged like an unoiled gate

as they

rested

for a bit

between

clouds

under

an oak

tree.

"He certainly makes you smile."

The words were carried
away on the breeze.

And so was

he.

011

"He's certainly no one you should
be friends with" they'd say!

"He won't even talk to the ordinary
people" they'd add!

Sam would
always have
to quiet him
in these moments.

He became
difficult and
far too hard
on himself.

But Sam was
the sparrow
of his day.

His mood
somewhat
softer
when he
spoke.

012

"He's lucky
he has someone
to understand him."

He heard
in a whisper
that pierced
through

the

crowd.

And it

made

him

smile

while

he

pretended

not

to

hear

a thing.

013

"The sun was
finally shining"

He groaned
in disappointment.

The rain always came
unexpectedly.

"The clouds
were miles away..."

He added,
wide stretched

and yawning,

as he woke

from the

afternoon

nap.

The day
had been
interrupted
by
nature
again.

"They'll pass."

Sam
assured him,
calmer
than
usual.

Understanding
his frustration.

"They always pass."

014

He's still
learning that Sam didn't have
to understand

to care.

"Why are you always so quiet?"

Especially

when he got

like this.

Sam said
in an unusually
unshining
voice.

He grew
even
quieter.

And blank in the face.

"You really don't have much sense do you."

Especially

when he got

like this.

Sam continued

with clouds

in his

eyes.

"I don't know..."

He said,

almost embarrassed,

breaking the tension
with a lightly lit laugh.

015

The muttering moved
               into tenseness.

     His internal conflict
                  could
             sometimes
                be seen by
        others.

    And Sam knew
            there was
                a reason
                    that he
             was
             calm with
        the tired
     look on
his face.

    Without eyes for the day,

             words

             seemingly

               passed

               right

               through
         him.

It was
        in this
        that the words
        with meaning lost
                their light.

But it was

            rare he had

these eyes,

            clouded

                        and

                        distant.

He smiled,
        and Sam surely was
                the sparrow of his day.

016

They walked
        in silence.

      His mind still perplexed.

Still

           pulsing

               in the dark.

      "It's being

able to

        understand

               a certain sort
of language."

He

inadvertently

      made Sam smile

          with his explanation.

"It's how

the wind

makes

music

through

these

branches."

Still perplexed.

He was

all the

more

nervous.

But
he
knew
Sam
understood.

017
"Not really
one thing
or the other"

He thought
      to himself
      in quick words.

      Looking at Sam
with a certain
curiosity.

Sam was
      standing half
      in the shadow
      of an old elm.

And

the unhinged
glance made him

    wonder
    with one
    eye
    squinting

        in the
        afternoon
        light.

"What are you gawking at?"

Sam asked

        half laughing.

"A sparrow..."

        He said

with a

        smile.

018

The

morning

grew

grey

as he

stared intently

and far

too hard.

Sam felt it.

He was
questioning
the sun's
radiance.

Sam often

tried to follow
his thoughts.

"You have owl eyes."

The phrase
    so sudden
    it was
       almost
         sharp.

    Sam smiled

                   and

         became
his

   sparrow.

019

The ground was
      yellow with
      damp
          leaves.

And
the puddles
      passed
      from white
          to brown.

As they walked
beneath the trees
      a certain silence
          fell between them.

"How did all this happen?"

The plainness
         of the question
hit him in
         the
         gut.

                              He didn't know.

And he definitely
didn't think about
it when Sam was
         around.

"Like leaves grow trees."

He said so wryly
it wasn't
         the words
                  that
                  Sam
                  understood.

020

He couldn't
concentrate
with
the
electric
hum.

It broke
his thoughts
and he knew
that Sam

couldn't
hear it.

He had
asked him
awkwardly
once
before.

So he smiled
half-cocked
and tried
to explain
again.

"It's not
that I hear
them.

I just know
  what they're
  saying."

He could read
the frustration
on his face.

But Sam
looked
for his
intention,

        and
              kissed
him.

021

They were
       in darkness
             and the street lights shone
                 in columns.

As their
       shadows
             became tall
       and danced
   in the
distance.

"We're beyond
the rising
and the falling."

He thought
     to himself
         in words
too soft
     to be
spoken.

Their smiles
     said it all
         anyway.

And

          they

          knew

the world

of things

          still
existed,

now just

          vaguely

darker.

As Sam
     became
          his star.

He became
his illumination.

022

He looked at him

probingly
for a
moment
and
found
it was
his
willing
suspension
of
disbelief
that
made
him
smile.

Sam loved
to pry at
his mind,
but the moon
was
still casting
shadows
and somehow
he noticed.

"Now you're
the one gawking!"

He
grinned,
and gave
a nudge.

He laughed
and Sam smiled
at the echo.

023

Reality was
    heavy
            and hardly
    at ease
            as black
                    apparitions
    ran through
            his mind.

"They're as
tangible as
the dark."

He explained.

Sam
never
knew
                                    his

voice
could
feel so
                                    absent

and he
didn't
know how
to respond
to his
                                    solitude.

The words were

        choked

                and

he

felt

        the tear

                        was

                        growing.

024
And the noise
    of the world
    bothered him.

"You're
completely
alone."

            A terrified
            rushing vanished
            in his ear.

But
    he felt
        ordinary
            when
            Sam was
                around.

A certain sense
of serenity followed
him and nothing
seemed to matter.

025

They were
      bathed
      in stars

            and

    walked

  in

                glory
      through
      the

        dim

      vertical
      lines
        of
          light

      and

      the faint

             illumination
             of
             the distant
             city

Sparrows into Owls
&
The World of Things

026

The sun sat on the city
    and an orange
    and yellow glow
      saturated
        the two of them,
              piercing
          the moment.

"The dog days
are beginning."

            He
          stated
          as a simple
          fact,
        dappled in radiance
      and dew,
       removing himself from what
    he intended.

     He was

        slightly insecure

          about the way

           he was.

He sat

on the bench,

the park

just barely vacant

of tricks and thieves.

Sam sat too.

And the world was

waking

in that moment as

they sat

in silence.

027

The two
    let the sun
       put
       distance

                          between
                          them

       as morning
broke
       into day.

Sam had obligations
and
the world was
       demanding.

He knew
       that this
              couldn't last.

The temporary nature
       only made sense.

Though

he
wanted it
to be
prolonged beyond
what
was

possible.

"It was..."

Stumbled
out of his
mouth as Sam
continued.

He would have
to remind himself
that Sam would
return.

028

Sleep was
 the

                              furthest

 thing
 from his mind
   as he managed
      the pangs of

   being

      a

 passionate man.

   The day was
     reduced
       to a lounge
         and all thoughts
           left him.

"It's important
to remember."

Sounded sharp

in the siren

of a passing

ambulance.

And he thought of what Sam
might
have said in this moment.

029

He would often talk
to himself.

"There's
a certain
continuity."

He said,
starkly

referencing

his newly found

friend.

"And it only stands to reason

that he

sees a certain

side of

me."

He continued,

remembering how

he often

removed

himself

from the situation

before

this

point.

"It's a tendency,
like breathing,

or

laughing."

He tried to

explain.

Standing
    in the instance,
        a separate segment,

    a

        point become line.

"But it all seems

    out of focus,

yet sharp

    and not

        so subtle."

030

It was
only in
comparison that
he could say
that the moment
had
worsened.

Sam
certainly
brought
something

out

of
him
and
the
world
was
lighter
as a

result.

The sun
peeked
in through
the window
above his bed.

And he saw

the dust

on its

suspended

journey.

And he

realized.

That was
exactly what
Sam did to him.

Shone,
and made
the world
of things
brighter.

031

The night came quickly
     and
     the world of things,
     the world
          Sam solidified,
               soon became vague.

Leaving less and less
     room for reason.

And he felt
     that
     Sam knew
          this.

And
he told himself
     his sparrow
          would return.

032

"There was
hell in his touch."

He thought to himself,

locked in the memory

of his continual return.

Sam's absence remained
in the shadowy

figures

of the world

of things.

And he knew
that he was
being irrational.

But Sam was
his sparrow,
and his star,
and his light.

033

He had
      made himself

           small,

     and discrete

          in
          his
          aching.

Swiftly
     his thoughts
     turned back
        to reality
        from
     the wandering
     of Sam's absence.

Tossing
     over himself
        in determination.

The fetid nature
of his
thoughts

was

plainly visible.

The light
beyond the
window panes
captured him
that night.

034

Vulnerable
    and far too
        willing.

He had
    grown
        use to
            the
            company.

Sam was
    at any
        given moment
            a certain
                cohesion
                and
                centrality.

Realizing
    that he was
        using him
            for coping.

The
electric buzz
        returned.

And he
felt as
though
he was
becoming
small
again.

"It's complicated..."

Sounded

        in the sigh

                of cheap
                        mattress

springs

        and sweat.

035

At times,
　　he knew
　　　　how childish
　　　　he was
　　　　　　being.

He had handled
　　the world
　　　　before he
　　　　　　met Sam.

Yet
　　the
　　　　situation
　　　　　　wasn't
　　　　　　　　the most
　　　　　　rational.

And it was
        only when
            he thought
                of how
                    brilliant
                        Sam

was

                    that
            his
                    absence
            also
        removed
    a certain
        clarity.

Reason
    returned
            and in an
                instant
            he grew
                into

                    his

                    aloneness.

036
"We're all cameras."

He thought
        as he tried
to understand.

"And sometimes we flash

and blind each other."

  He had felt
        blinded by Sam.

                  It was
                  in this
                moment
       that his self
             returned.

And the world

        of things was

                fluid again.

This was

his continuity.

And he thought

about the

difference.

And the meaning

of a sparrow.

037

The knock
    on the door

                elevated
                his existence

     in a moment
     of child-like
          excitement.

His footsteps cried,

"Careful."

    in the creeks
      of the uneven
        kitchen floor.

     The peep
     hole taunted
him
with the possibility
     that it wasn't Sam.

Surely it truly

had to be

though.

Sam's brilliance shone.

And his light cast away
the shadows
that

found

their way

into

the

apartment.

038

The opening door
    created
    a rift,

            and

        the pressure

  produced

        nearly

         killed him.

He anticipated
    Sam's glowing
      radiance.

Cross-sections
    of
    a
wryly smile
    revealed
his self,

         as the gap
    made Sam

      visible.

"I missed"

He wasn't

even

allowed

to trail

off

this

time.

Sam kissed him.

"Me too."

039a
"It's only
in our nature."

He started,

trying to seed
Sam
into

conversation.

Sam was

distracted

and for a moment

seemed

distant.

For once

the roles

were reversed.

And
        he knew
      those eyes
    of longing
  too well.

Sam wanted
    to say

something.

      Reserved
    and unwilling
  to ask Sam
the apparent
     question.

He continued.

Ignoring

the obvious.

039b

"We are animals after all."

Through
the

pause
in his eyes,

"I care about you."

Sam blurted

out,

unfinished
and
far

less

refined

than

usual.

Sam looked slightly
removed
and
uneasy.

Confused
by the plainness,
he
knew
Sam was

hiding.

"I care about you too."

Unwillingly,
both knew
that more
had just
been said.

040

He was playing
Otis Redding,

and Sam was
clearly

curious

why.

"It isn't every day you hear this."

Sam was

staring

at

the

spinning

vinyl.

As the sun

captured his face

the dust

had

formed

a

notion
of

splendor.

The song

finished

and

Sam

lifted

the needle.

"Let's go."

He nodded.

And they went.

Together.

041
The noise

of the crowd

created an air

of

privacy

that

they

both

often

strived

for.

The

        market

always

           seemed

   to have

      this

         though.

And they passed

      through it

        with relative

   ease.

Unnoticed.

And without

incident.

Sam was

      still distant,

        his mind

    still pulsing,

        but the world of

things

              solidified.

      And Sam was
        still

            his

sparrow.

042

Sam seemed to be
      easing
           into the day,

     notions
        of clarity

         surrounded
      the two
         of them.

       And he noticed
       Sam returning
       with a smile.

Determined
      to understand
       the previous

distance,
      he allowed
         his
         tongue
         to slip.

"What were you..."

He stopped

himself

in the middle

of curiosity.

Sam smiled

and

ignored

the murmur.

043

He saw
    that Sam's
    eyes were
        Sahara
            blue.

    And he could
    hardly help
        but notice
        the hue's
            piercing
            quality.

"They're a desert."

        He thought
        through
        the
        amazement.

And he
would often
get lost in them.

Sam was
          looking in
                    the window
                              of an old
                                        antique shop.

And they reflected
in the glass a time
          that neither
          would ever know,
                    but longed for.

                              And they remembered
                    times they couldn't
          have possibly had.

044a

"How are you doing?"

Sam asked

with his

sincerity
showing
like the
white

of

his
teeth.

He knew Sam
didn't mean
right now

or even today

for that matter.

"There isn't much."

He knew

that he couldn't
lie
but he really was

used to this.

It was
all too
common.

"It's not the lightning, or the thunder.

It's the camera
flashes that get
to me."

He continued
in low breath.

044b

"I'm a camera too though."

He knew Sam cared.

And he appreciated
that Sam never tried
to fix anything about him.

Though there
was little to fix
when Sam was
                around.

                And
                he knew
                that his
                sparrow
                was swiftly
                becoming

                        an owl.

And he knew,
like Sam,
he couldn't

                hide
                for
                long.

045
At times Sam thought

of him as Janus.

He saw the duality

within
him as being
both ahead and
behind him.

It wasn't
simple.

He knew

it couldn't be.

"There are
definitely
two of him."

Sam thought,
recalling the times

he looked at him

without him

knowing.

And saw passed
the stern exterior.

Into a more

slack

side of him.

With
discretion in his
eyes,
Sam
knew
he was hiding.

And he was
good at it.

046
They were

on their way back

to the apartment

when he

noticed

that Sam never
took the

side
streets.

And their shadows

intermingled

as they walked
into the
sun.

In a moment
of childlike levity,
Sam switched

directions,

walking backwards
to see him
more plainly.

"Well
this isn't
any better."

Sam made
him smile

in the light
of two suns.

047
The door was
        a decision.

And a return

                to fluidity
                and shadow.

The sound of the keys

                                almost
                            echoed down
                            the silent
                            hallway.

                            He
                        thought
                            of Sam's
                        continual return
                as a series of goodbyes,
                                and
                                he
                                had
                                to
                                stop
                                it.

"Coffee or tea."

All
              he
                         could

trickle
              out
                         to

keep
                         Sam

from
                         leaving.

"Do you have black tea?"

                    Sam asked
                    with a smile.

"Yes."

                    And they
                    listened
                    to Wagner
                    on the radio.

048

He lived

in the slums

and Sam
had to
take
a train

to see him.

"How did you end up here?"

Sam sipped on his
tea,
forgetting it
was
still too
hot.

"Just like you did."

He wasn't good
at small talk.

And he didn't know
why Sam was
making it.

"We walked here together."

He continued,
        speaking
through

                a smile.

"What do you think Wagner
meant by 'Twilight of the Gods'?"

Sam realized
        that this was
                different.

And they
        both sipped
                black tea
        in between
the words
        that hadn't
                been
        said.

049

Hours went by,
 and both
  of them
   realized

that neither
 were
getting

much

sleep

lately.

"Do you want to go to bed?"

Sam asked,

seeing his

eyelids

dance.

"You should stay..."

Sam made him small,

but he smiled

        as Sam nodded.
                                They

                    both

        stood

up.

        And

                Sam
                                followed

                                him
                        into
            the

    dark

        and

        dimly
    lit
                                bedroom.

050
They were

lost

within

the

faint

illumination

of

the

once

distant

city,

and

the

vertical

lines

now

crossed

them

while

they

were

caught

in

darkness

but

shone

with

glory.

Owls into Ghosts
&
Within the Distant City

051
There was

cotton

in the air

out

the
window

as

he sat

in the

sun

drinking

coffee.

Sam was

still sleeping,

and the day

had

with it

the

complications

of
the

morning

after.

But he was

    still locked

      in

           the darkness,
     and
             the
    indiscretions

  of

    passion.

The pangs of
          being
           a passionate
          man

     were

        well worth

   the night where
                  the city

             seem

   didn't

    so
    distant.

052a

He usually
took
them
at
night.

And
he
realized
that

perhaps

he was
enthralled
in
the
moment.

And
that
this
had

completely

left
his
mind.

A torrid wave

       passed

right through him

                  as he
                  was pushed

      to the counter.

He took them

      without water

        and he tasted

     the bitter

     alkaloid flavor

     that

       comforted

               his
     worst
     fears.

052b

Sam hadn't yet woken,
    and he knew
        he would be tired,
            and without eyes
              for the day.

        There was
      nothing
he could do
    now.

Though he had
    gotten
        good
            at it,

he could
    hardly hide
        for long.

He had
to come out
and allow
the day to come.

He now knew that Sam cared.

"Well this is interesting..."

He thought

in

a bland excitement.

"In exoneration
and in crime alike,
and in love."

053

Sam awoke,
and they noticed
a distinction.

It arose with the opening
of Sam's

eyes.

And slid
a blank slate
onto their face.

He didn't know what to say
and he

feared

stagnation.

Resentment.

And absence.

Looking at Sam
          with hesitation
                                              he

          saw

that he was

staring out the window
          at the suspended
                              cotton.

And he knew.

"Coffee?"

          A natural conclusion
               to a revolution
                    bore the night before.

"Sure."

     Sam had warmth in his voice.

          He knew.

     And they started the day together.

054
Differentiated

in the most

subtle way.

He felt himself fade.

And he knew that today

was

going to be not nearly as

easy

as others had

been,

as easy as Sam

so seemingly made

them.

What brought him into the

world

shared by others,

tore him

away

in an

instant.

And he knew differentiated would

soon be not

nearly

as

subtle.

And he only hoped that Sam

wouldn't ask why.

The answer was a black
spot of embarrassment.

And he was
prideful.

055a

He wasn't

                hiding

        as well today,

      and though he tried,

                Sam saw.

      Pouring coffee
            into a teacup,
      Sam allowed
            his curiosity to swell.

"How did you sleep last night?"

    He starred
    into his coffee
    for a moment.

      "You look tired."

He cared,
and he knew
that halfway
wasn't going
to be enough.

055b

"I slept fine, Sam."

Slipped

out

of his

mouth

without looking up,

or allowing himself

to

stutter.

"I simply forgot my life last night.

As well as the importance of time."

Sam was

slightly

confused,

but he allowed

it to pass.

Sam often let

these

comments

pass.

056

He was

a day

in December
in the midst
of the dog days
of summer.

Suddenly,

remote

and

without

thrall.

Sam wasn't at all lost

in the clouds
of his
eyes

and knew.

"You'll get better at telling me these things?"

Sam said
in the most stern,
yet caring
way
imaginable.

"I imagine I will."

Creaked

out

of

him

like

a

leak

in

an

old

tire.

"I apparently

just lost myself

somewhere last

night

you'll

have

to forgive me."

057

His heart was
    graceless.

      And it was

      moments like
      this that he was
      lost to his discretion.

        Privacy
    in this modern world,
        and in love,
        just doesn't exist.

    Something had to be said.

But those pills had left him listless.

      It was
    why they sent him to bed.

But the consequential reality,
and the universal connection
    made it mandatory.

"I forgot to take my medication."

His pride
was a little lost on Sam.

But there were complications

in far simpler happenings.

Sam smiled.

"Alright!

Perhaps we'll just
            be lost today."

Somehow a sparrow was
all Sam could be,
even
with
his
owl
eyes.

058
To him

in this state,

Sam

shone

like a

roman candle.

Streaks across

the sky

without discretion

or

compromise.

But the world

of things

became vague before

a falling curtain.

It was
the importance of timing
     and of the grace of

      men

           who didn't

know his life

                 or

situation.

                    Sam was

           learning this

            in the

                  flares

of illumination.

059

"Leaving lefts aside..."

He said stonily

with a smile,

"Today is finally starting to feel right, Sam."

It was relative

of course,

and lazy.

Sam had sat on

the couch

and positioned
himself behind

him.

Leaning back,
            he was

secure in Sam's

chest.

They drank

their coffee.

And watched

the window.

With

            the sounds
    of their voices
            echoing like

        Wagner.

060

Sam saw
　　　that he didn't
　　　　　want to be
　　　　　saved.

　　　There was
　　　　　little saving
　　　　　　　to do it seemed
　　　　　　　anyway.

　　　　　He was
　　　independent,
and prideful
　　　to a fault.

Though without
　　　want or need
　　　　　of a savior,
　　　　　　　Sam somehow
　　　　　saw this as proof
of a weakness.

He saw that he was

compensating

for that black dog

chasing him.

And all he

wanted

was

for him

to forget

that he was

running.

Or

to forget

that the black

dog existed

at all.

061
"Does this happen often?"

Sam was
curious,

      and far

           more

        comfortable
with the situation

          now.

Leaning back

         into Sam

     a little

harder,

      he sighed.

"If it happens ever,

it happens too often."

There was
exhaustion

in his words.

They trailed off

in a typical

manner.

"But No."

He was

diligent

with

necessity.

"I am typically good
with myself."

062

Neither gave

> the night before
> a second thought.

> > It was
> > > just the new
> > > state of things.

> > It was
> > > the natural
> > > progression.

> And Sam wasn't
> even put off
> > by what transpired
> > the morning after.

He cared.

And he knew
he managed
himself.

There was
no need.

There was
no desperation.

There was

nothing

but the

cotton

in the air,

a nap on

the couch,

and quiet
conversation.

063

It was
      in
      the rebellion
         against

              his
              childhood

           that he didn't
              want a martyr.

And
      he
         often
           warned
           against
              guilt.

      There was
           little to be said
              when
           faced with
           apology,
           though he often
           tried
              to
              make
           things right.

He couldn't help the
way he was.

He
seemingly just
couldn't stop.

So Sam
saw him
without
the rebellion he
portrayed.

Or the notion of
his ideals.

Owl eyes had certainly
become Sam's
blessing
in the vagueness
of the world of things.

064

He was
　　a defect of the city.

　　　　And his sparrow

　　　　　　suffered simplicity

　　　　　　　　of heart.

　　　　　　But lying deeply
　　　　　　into Sam's chest
　　　　　　reminded
　　　　　　him
　　　　　　of the night
　　　　　　before.

　　Suddenly

　　　　there was
　　　　　　fluidity in this
　　　　　　seemingly
　　　　　　　　increasingly
　　　　　　　　vague world.

And his hand
reached as if muscle
memory told it
where to go.

As he thought

in hopeless

expressions

words

that he would

never say aloud.

Or admit to
even have thought.

But there
was
class in this
frightful condition.

And
hope.

065

He jostled

    himself

        into

       position.

      Side by side only
       seemed right.

    They were reflections
         of each other.

    His head fell on Sam's

         shoulder
       in comfort

and exhaustion.

       Clarity

    didn't seem

      to matter

   with

       a hand

    on his

   thigh.

And his

         fingers

meandering

               between

      Sam's

chest and arm.

There

        was

        little

to

             disguise.

And neither
      dared to mind
the new state
        of things.

066

It was
　　　　about the time
　　　　　　　　that he often turned
　　　　　　　　　　on public
　　　　　　　　　　　radio.

　　　　　　　　He felt
　　　　　　　　　　connected
　　　　　　to the world
　　　　　　　　as a whole
　　　　　　because of it.

　　　　　　　　　　　　Somehow

　　　more
　　cosmopolitan.

　　　　　　　But this was
　　　　　　　a microcosm.

　　　　　　　　　　　　And

　　　　　　isolated
　　　didn't
　　　　　　seem nearly as bad.
　　　　　　　　　　　　With
　　　　　　Sam.

There was

little about the

world
that he cared

about.

Cold coffee.

And silence.

And

beams

of light
through

the window.

The world
of things
was
changing
though

the forms

stayed

the same.

067

He picked up

a book

from off the table.

Reading in a voice

kept for poetry.

He looked at Sam.

"You are terrifying.

And strange.

And beautiful."

Sam didn't

expect him

to be so

piercing

with someone

else's words.

"Something not everyone knows how to love."

He carried on with words

like a ragged thespian.

Sam smiled.

And whispered loudly.

"Perhaps you're a bit confused today."

068
Somehow

it was

midday.

And the cotton
had drifted from the air.

And both had become distracted.

Sam allowed

his concern to show

in quick sentences.

"How are you feeling?"

He had to refocus.

He

hadn't

been

thinking

about

his well-being.

"Distinct."

The only word that came to mind.

Though
not
what
Sam
was
looking for,

he smiled

and sighed.

069

They were

        discerning each other

            with wide strokes

of ego and thinly

          veiled boundaries.

Their minds were

          racing in the silence

of the apartment.

And the soft tension

          that was built

the night before.

          Fighting the urge

to peacefully die

            in

this moment.

    He got up.

Turned on the radio.

And returned to Sam.

"NPR is something of a bad habit."

He smiled
with wry
rebellion.

"I'm addicted to being well-informed."

And
something
told him that

Sam

suffered

similar

affliction.

070
Though the goal
of the day
was
to do nothing
at any cost.

They had to sustain
their self somehow.

Hunger was

a word like

domestic.

And neither
liked shopping.

"Ramen or rice?"

He thought out loud

without shame.

"Neither!"

Sam wasn't trying

to starve,

but

something

had to be done here.

Both became aware
that leaving was
now the only
option.

And domestication

instantly

became

a

new

destination.

071

They

    hadn't

        thought

            ahead.

Yesterday's clothes

        were still

           in the

bedroom.

Dressing seemed to be
      the chore
         of the
         hour.

"Do you
have a shirt
I can wear?"

      Sam knew it
      was going to
      be tight.

But he didn't account
                    for a closet
                    of smalls.

Slightly amused.

                        He ran
            to the
            bedroom.

"Here!"

                    There was
                        a
                        childlike
                        quality
                        that Sam
                        just
            discovered.

        And
        perhaps
                this
                    was
                            more
                            than
                            newness
                            and wry.

072

They didn't care what

people

thought of them today.

They had a silent

promise

to each other that trounced

public
opinion.

"What are you hungry for?"

Sam asked as he became
domesticated in an instant.

"Something edible, Sam."

He didn't want to
respond without
knowing his options.

"Let's forage and explore."

A calm

excitement

overcame

them.

And

he

forgot

that

he

hadn't

had

eyes

for

the

day.

073

They caught each
        other in
        glances
        as they
        quickly
        dressed
        and moved
        toward the
              door.

        He touched
        Sam's arm
in guidance
and care.

And Sam reached
        for the small
        of his back

              to push
              him

              out
              of the
              apartment.

Opening

the door,

they saw

certainty

and

domestication.

He thought

of

the

threshold

as

a

distant

Rubicon.

And

Sam

as

Caesar.

"All too Roman…"

He thought

between the teeth

of Sam's smile.

And they exited,

together.

074
Closing

the door,

they left

their heart

of

seclusion

behind.

It was

lost

in the

vagueness

of the world
of things.

And they

    entered,

        with hesitation,

    the distant city

of the other.

    It wasn't

        without goal

            though.

    And both
    intended
    to return.

        And to leave

this all behind

once again.

    Together.

075
They

wandered
through

the
faint

illumination
within

the
once

distant
city.

Passing
vertical

lines
of

walking
light.

Still
caught
in
darkness.

Still
shining

with
glory.

And
victorious.

Ghosts into Children
&
An Empire of Thought

076

Too often he was
         lost to the empire
               of his thought.

An exile in a vast
         expanse that went on
               by itself without rulers.

Sam saw this in him as they walked
down the street.

"Sometimes you're
like these buildings."

Sam said.

Being
      uncharacteristically
                  poetic.

"And there's people
looking out of your windows."

He couldn't help
but be slightly
amazed at the words
Sam decided to use.

"Are they happy people, Sam?"

There was
enough
being said
in the moment.

Sam smiled,
and looked ahead.

077
There was

a difference

in the silences

they created

between each

other.

They weren't
at all
like the
awkward
pauses
they
both
fought
as they walked
within the distant city
of the other.

They were quiet
understandings.

And unspoken
thoughts
intended to be
kept secret.

And both knew
this in
similarity.

"It isn't far!"

Words that jut out
in surprise of the moment
they shared.

"I'm not concerned."

Sam hadn't intended
to allow that thought
to escape.

But it did.

078
Neither

thought

of discretion

as being

necessary.

It was

a modern

world after

all.

And
society
was
changing.

Had changed.

And people were
only partially
appalled at
such behavior.

They passed

their shadows

in the
noonday

sun with

the others.

"It's at the end of the block!"

He allowed
another
concession
of territorial
knowledge
to erupt.

"I'm not that concerned."

This time,

intending
to attract,

Sam
allowed
a laugh
to shine
as he smiled.

He enjoyed the walk.

079

He was

      feeding ghosts

           with

              his

           thoughts

           about

           the

           night

           before.

           Nothing
           needed
           to be said.

           There was

           no discomfort.

           And not a thing

           emerged

           as urgently wrong.

           But nonetheless.

He fed ghosts

through

distant

reverie

and

reserved

attraction.

They were almost

at their destination.

Walking

in silence.

Detracted
    in the
    moment,
    he was
no longer
hungry.

Or wanting.

Or wry.

080

Domestication
    had become
    the destination.

           So with
           its arrival,

                  it was
                  no longer
                  fantasy
                  and
                  fairy
                  tale

          that
          they
          found
          their

selves
within,
if it ever
was
at all.

Somehow
the ideals

about
the other

were
dispelled

with the fact
that they

were both
human.

There was
commonality

in the struggle
against hunger,

and for love.

And in this,
they became
the same
species.

Undifferentiated.

081

They both
        awaited the swift
        return of the world
                within the other.

                Away
                from
                those
                wandering
                this once distant city.

                Though they too wandered,
                they did not completely belong.

                They entered the grocery store.

                In defiance of what they
                intended for each other.

                And their selves.

                It wasn't at all
                what they
                imagined.

                But it was
                comfortable.

                And right.

Though
nothing
could return
to the disillusioned
and the fanciful.

Now
with
spots
of clarity,
both simply
knew.

082

Fluorescent lights
        and artificial
        strangers.

        The
        aisles
        were filled
        with people.

                In
                rows
                of carts
                like food
        stocked on
        shelves for
        everyone
        to see
        clearly.

        Suddenly,
        in the world
        of abundance,
        they were struck
        dumb and clueless.

        "What are you hungry
                for, Sam?"

He managed

amid the disdain

for the setting.

"Not ramen or rice."

Now Sam was

the wry one

in strokes

of humor

laced

sense.

He usually

came here

in the desolate

hours of the morning.

And he wasn't happy.

083

He was
      reminded
           of why
           he fell victim
                to seclusion.

But he
didn't allow
                it to shine
                through
                the clouded
                eyes
      they
      shared.

Sam knew
      that
      he felt
      displaced.

And ravenous
      to a point.

"How about soup
      and bagels?"

Trying to decide
seemed to be
a matter that
Sam was
determined
to resolve.

"Tomato soup?"

Realizing
his fetid nature
in situations that
he didn't appreciate.

He smiled.

And they knew
that domestication was
only a vacation
in the distant city
of the other.

084
There was
        a premonition

                of love

                        in

                        the

                moment.

                And
                they
                knew
                each
                other's

                humanity

                        while

        fighting

                their domestication.

While they

      gathered

      their reasons

      for leaving

    the world within

    the other.

They managed their way
to the cashier,
and were
relieved to find that she
      was pleasant.

And dapper.

"Is this all for today?"

    She queried
    in a mouse of
    a voice.

      They nodded.

    And with
    a swipe of
  a card they
were released.

085
Being

children

of their time,

they were restless

and irreverent.

Ill-equipped
for the most
banal places
and moments
it seemed.

But this notion
of the independent
self didn't keep
them from
each other.

And the awkward
condescension
        found
        in the typicality of
their everyday life didn't
keep them

        from their ideals.

They were young,
        and free to be lost
                within the other.

Youthful indiscretions
had made them
this way.

                Making their way
                        to the exit,
                they left
                the domestic
        behind.

But only
        for a moment.

086
The cotton

had

fallen

into

the

air

with

suspended

radiance

again.

Each tuft glowed
in the afternoon sun,
and allowed itself
                to be
                        taken fully.

"I wish we were small enough!"

                                He
                        allowed
                a childlike fantasy
        to expose who he was.

                Or who he
                        wanted to be.

"we could float
and a puddle
would be
an ocean."

                        Feeling slightly
                silly at this point.

        He became grey tongued,
        and tucked himself
        into his head.

Sam

was carrying

the grocery bag

and knew that he

was holding back.

"It would be nice
to be small enough."

Sam

was amused

at the distinct

difference between

then and now.

They had clearly

left the others behind.

087

They were human
    now
    and
    prone
    to such
    irrational
    behavior.

        It seemed
        distinctions
        were being
        made without
        consent.

        Or
        regard
            for
            the
        other.

        But in the midst
        of the distance
        of
        the
        city
        of
        the
        other,
        distinctions just
        needed to be made.

Restless
and
irreverent
were
all they
could
be.
And
the
nuances
of being
who
they
were
all but
left
them
wanting.

Seeing
each
other
in their
broad
strokes.
Knowing
ideals
had been
cast aside,
they
continued
to walk.

088

He

    hadn't

        heard

            his
            shadows,
            or the electric
            hum at all lately.

                    And
                    in his
                    own way
                    this was
                  a glad
                abnormality.

                It seemed
              nothing ever
           changed
       in the world
          of things
             and
             distance.

            But Sam
            either drove
            them off,
         or made him
    forget completely.

Both
were
welcome.

And
wanted.

He was
        finding himself
        attached to this
        shared reality
he had with
Sam.

        Disregarding
                the common
                urge to get up
                and walk away
                that he often
        had by now.

He knew.

And they
became
children.

089

In moments like this,
      they both had to fight
      the blatant urge to fully
      romanticize the other.

          A commonality
          among lovers.

          And though
          they tried.

          It wasn't
          the lack
     of distinctions
     between the two
     of them that kept
          them intact.

            It was
            because
            they didn't
            need each
                other.

Or at least
not in ways
that either
would
admit.

It was
that they
compared
the other to
the rest
of their
world.

And simply
found that it
was better
this way.

090
They continued

walking

through

the slums

with dirty

streets.

And
strange
people.

The world within
the other only
blocks away.

And they
noted
the
sanctuary
of the
apartment
in silence.

Though

           he was

    used to

             this,

Sam wasn't

           in

    the least.

And

      saw

         the

            others

  as foreign.

            And lost.

          Music blared

      from
  a passing
  car.

       And the mundane
became
  their adventure.

091

The true
      distinctions
      were between
             them
             and
             the
             others.

The ones
the distant city
grasped in cold
embrace.

      Without
         them
             knowing.

Their
distinctions
made this
clear to
them.

      Though
        they
           had
             to
             assert
          to their
        selves.

And to each other.

That
the world
they shared
wasn't just
created
    that
    morning
in the awkward
pauses of coffee.

Sunshine.

And cotton.

 That

it

            was

   just

as

 distantly

         inevitable

     as
the

   rain.

092

"We are beings
       towards death,
              and that's all
                     we are."

       Welcome words
              that burst through
                     the silent streets.

       Sam didn't
              understand
                     immediately.

      He didn't often
              quote philosophy.

"But we have
desires in the face
                     of this death."

      Sam didn't
            see where
                 this came
                     from.

        It was
                  sudden.

And
            seemed
               harsh.

"And because of this,
            I must feel the
                        fire of my
                                    soul."

He looked at Sam
            directly and smiled
                        with intent.

"That was
                        interesting."

Sam saw this
                        as an allowance.

And he knew
            that he was
                        finally comfortable.

So they
            continued
                        to walk.

093

They were men
of resentment
in this world
of things.

And
the distant city
cried to them
with the others
they knew.

So there was a
certain continuity
which defined the two
of them in relation
to these others.

And though
they felt hidden.

It was
only in the bad faith
of the world.

In this they
reluctantly gave up
their transcendence.

"I think I left
the radio on,
Sam."

A stark
contrast to
the moment
just before.

Sam agreed.

And
they
approached
the
world

within
the other.

094

He had
    a torrid
        tune stuck
            in his head
                again.

            It wasn't
            often that
            he enjoyed
            musicals.

        But Sondheim made
him smile every time.

He hummed
out the words.

        And was
        surprised
        that Sam knew
            the tune as well.

        They approached
the stoop of the
apartment building.

"I'm so hungry, Sam."

Weak words that
were wholly empty.

Simply meant
to fill a gap.

"Me too."

It wasn't
the response
that put him off.

It was
how Sam
said it.

He wasn't
responding
to the same
statement.

They walked
up the stairs
toward a wide
wooden door.

095

Though
Sam carried
the groceries.

He also
opened
the door
with the
class of
a gentleman
who too often
thought
of love.

Independent
and not yet
used to such
behavior.

He gave out
a look of ridicule
and romance.

There

was

a front

he was

pushing

through

with the

threshold

as an ivory

wall.

    And he allowed
    the pressure
    to build
    in suspense
    of the moment.

        Nervously.

        He smiled.

096

As he

    walked
    through
    the doorway
    he remembered
          Sartre.

"Secret and deep,
    and comes from
        far away."

        Somehow it
        seemed to fit.

        Everything
      seemed to fit.

And he allowed Sam
      to follow him
back into the world
within the other.

Away from
the cold
distant
city.

        To eat soup.

        And bagels.

And allow
    the day
    to simply
    happen.

    There was
    a transit in
    progress
    that both
were unaware
of completely.

As they
    swallowed
    the suns
    of each
other in their
minds.

As they
walked
up to the
apartment
together.

097

They

somehow
spoke of life.

Of their life
with one
another.

And it didn't
seem that either
minded how they
implied a future.

It was
just the
state of
things
now.

The excursion
left them wanting
something more
of the other.

In blatant
disregard
    for reason,
    there was
        now an
        expectation.

              And

           though

        it was

      created

    that

morning.

It was

    and it

        seemed

           to persist.

098

The stairs
    seemed to be
    welcomed as they
        knew what the rest
        of the day would bring.

    They wouldn't have to leave.

                And saw that
                the other was
            a warm comfort
            of willingness.

    A calmness subdued
    the two of them.

    And nothing
    seemed to
    matter.

As they

disregarded

    their hopes

    and their fears

       of the world

       they didn't need

          anything but

            the other

            in this moment.

            Especially
            this
        moment.

    As they walked
up to another door.

Not so wide.

And not
so wooden.

099

The key was
      trapped
      in the hole
      for a second.

      And the resistance
      reminded him of life.

    There

                 was

        nothing

                    to

   expect

            from

                Sam.

             Except

         that

      he

  would

         be

           there.

That he wanted
to be there.

But they both
knew that it could
end at any moment.

But neither wanted
this to happen.

It didn't make sense.

They were
something
substantial.

And building.

And they knew
they could become
something great.

100

They

had

wandered

in

search

of

illumination

within

the

distant

city

of

the

other.

But
they
had
become
the
vertical
lines
of
walking
light.

As
they
had
fought
in
darkness,
but
shone
with
glory.

Victory

was

all

they

knew.

Children into Lovers
&
The World Within the Other

101

They

    entered
        the
        world
        within
           the
           other
           with
           ease.

                And
                with
                the
                notions
                of their
                ideals
                still
                intact.

        Domestication
        hadn't ruined
        the romance
        of the moment.

Or imposed on
the other.

He's grey eyed.
And beautiful…"

He

couldn't

help but

note the

clarity

of

the

glance.

And they
could all
but resist
the dialogue
they'd never
share.

They simply
smiled at the
reciprocation.

102

He

came
from
a long
line
of

                                    martyrs.

            And
            little
            did
            he
            know
            that
            Sam

                                    was

            an emotional

            creature.

There were
just blind spots
in their eyes when
it came to each other.

Another commonality
among lovers.

But

this

didn't

matter

in the

world

within

the other.

There
was
little
care
in
their
distinctions.

      And

                  in

the

      shadows

           they cast

                together.

103

The kitchen
was
a wasteland.

So,
they
carried
their
oasis
in a brown
paper bag
and set it
on the
counter.

Gently
Sam
reached
in with
eagerness.

And anticipation.

And pulled
out a large
can of
tomato
soup.

And a
half-dozen
bagels.

They were
both incredibly
hungry.

"Where would I find a pan?"

Sam was
more than eager
it seemed.

"I'm sure I'm looking at one."

He looked
at Sam
in admiration.

Then pointed
to a cupboard.

104

They hadn't
    been comfortable
        in each other.

        Yet it
        seemed
        as though
        domestication
        was far from
        a simple
        vacation.

                The world
            within the other
            was becoming
            cold in an array
                    of reality.

        And
        the
        distant
        city
            was
                    closing in
                        around

    them.

                Distinctions
            needed to
        be made.

To
    keep
      the
        other

distinctions

          that
      kept
   them
  from
the

        others.

They were selfish.

105

Sam opened

      and poured

           the can of soup

     into a pan he found

            in the lonely

        cupboard.

It hadn't
been used
yet.

     The tag was
     still on the
     handle.

        And it
        wreaked
        of thrift-market.

"You're a sweetheart, Sam."

     Honey words
     without the
     bees of life.

"Should I
     cut the bagels?"

An attempt

to try rang

through

too easily.

"No.

                They'll be fine."

Like so many

other things

left alone.

106

He leaned up
    against the cold
        counter.

Sam's back was
turned as he
    focused on
    the stove.

                Quietly.

He
stared
    into
    the
back of
    Sam's
        head.

And
    he felt
the cold
    from
the
    open
window
    on his
neck.

Something
    had
    changed.

And though

summer

had

arrived.

Sam was

a day in

December.

Bright

but

cold.

107

"Can you get the bowls out?"

Something was
on Sam's mind.

"Sure..."

He felt a tension
that didn't exist
that morning.

They fell from
the grace of
the night
before.

Lovers often
fall from grace
in the distant
city of the
other.

He set the bowls next to the stove.

And Sam poured in the soup.

And they walked to the living room.

And sat on the couch in silence.

108

Sipping soup
in silence in the
awkwardness
of the new
day.

In the new
      moment of
            the new day.

      Things
      were
      changing.

      Quickly.

      And
      without
regard.

He was
            anxious
     inside
        himself.

And he knew the signs.

This wasn't his first time.

Not at all was this his first time.

"What are you thinking, Sam?"

He smiled.

And Sam

forced

one.

109

With the way
  Sam loved.

        He was
        a war machine
            in 1941.

And

              it

left

                    him

        air

                    raided.

In rubble.

                    And
        wanting
                    more.

    "I'm just tired..."

    Sam wasn't good at lying.

But he suspended his
disbelief in light of
current circumstance.

"We didn't sleep much."

Though he thought
that this was
the point.

"I'm sure you'll
        sleep better tonight."

                    And

        he

                                    was

sure

                        that

                                                he

        was

                        sure.

110

Sam was
    asserting his
        dominance in
        stretches of silence
            that made him strive.

    It seemed
    hopeless
    at times.

        But the communication
    was fading into spurts of
    perfectly
    functional
    conversation
    with quiet
    shadows.

        He didn't
        realize that
     this was
     what he
     dreamed
   about in the
   years before
         with
      lonely
    lovers.

Sam was
just another
lonely lover.

111

The apartment
　　was silent.

But the radio
proved to be
an unwitting
　　savior.

Without distracting
Sam's dominant
structure.

He attracted
attention.

As he stood to
switch on NPR.

He saw that
the cotton was
locked in the
wind again.

But the air
seemed
empty.

Clouds
rolled in.

And he remembered
that this was
common.

And he
watched
as it began
to rain.

112

He watched
    out the window.

        As the raindrops
        weighed down
        the cotton.

      And removed
      its freedom.

  It could no
  longer fly.

      And he
      knew that
      this was
      what was
      happening.

        They were
        raining on
        each other.

          And for
          a moment
          he couldn't
          help but stare
          at the white
          streets with
          the once
          free tufts.

Distinctions were being made.

And he no longer knew his place.

"We're cotton, Sam."

Sam smiled.

113

He turned
    the radio
        down.

      Just
      enough
        to be
        heard.

      So that
      conversation
        was still
          possible.

        He didn't
      want Sam
    to feel that
he was being
      lost in the quiet
        sounds.

    Quietly.

    He attracted
Sam's attention
    by sitting closer
      to him than he
        was before.

Sam looked up.

But without a word
he continued to eat.

Amazed at
what was
happening.

He began
to eat again.

Quietly.

114

The silences
    between them
        became the
            awkward pauses
                that they had
            with the others.

        Now there was
no difference.

        Now they were
           just the same
                as anyone else.

           Imposters
        could come
and the world
wouldn't be
    any different.

        Or at least that's
how Sam was
making him feel.

Disposable.

Used up.

And old.

115
He knew

that this

wasn't

right.

And thought
that perhaps
he was being a
little irrational.

He
thought
that perhaps
he wasn't
seeing the
world quite
as right as
he should.

He thought
     that perhaps
     his medication
     was causing
     the world
     to fade
     again.

          But he was
          convinced
          that Sam was
          acting differently.

     That Sam
     had somehow
     changed.

          The world
               had suddenly
          become more
               clear.

          And
          far
          more
          cold.

116

Frantic stoicism
    rushed over him.

        In response
        to the day.

        In response
        to the way
            Sam was
            turning him
into a quiet
victim.

      He couldn't
      let this happen.

            He was
                fine.

            He knew
            Sam was
                fine.

            And he knew
            that everything
            had to be
                fine.

Quiet
conversations
      played over
      in his head.

      And he
        knew that
   something
   had
to be done.

117

"The city hasn't
yet made me hard."

He thought in bright

words that he

couldn't

let go.

"Sam is an
iron pillar."

He
looked
at Sam

in a different light
and lost himself
for a moment.

"And somehow
he thinks that he
is saving me."

Though
        true,

        there are
                no martyrs

    in the world
        within the
                other.

                    But he

                    knew

                    that Sam

            had found

            his self

    on a cross of his

    own creation.

    Unwittingly

                    or

        otherwise.

And
he knew
    that Sam
        had realized
          the same.

    He knew
that
Sam must
have
    realized
    the same.

"This is something
of a last supper."

Slipped from
the mind of the
most doubting
Thomas.

118

The difference was
     in the subtleties
     of the touch and
          of soft words,
          and in the tacit
     sensations that they
     both knew they had.

               These
               were
               gone.

        Hours had
        created
             a desert
               within
        their
        world.

And even
        though
             Sam was
        a second sun
that lit his life.

He was
cold.

And
distinctly
alone
in
a
distant
city.

Without
others.

119

Quiet indecision
    dominated the room.

    Quiet distinctions
        clearly had been made.

        Quiet words
            left unspoken
            floated through
            the air over an
            uneven kitchen
            floor.

And the coffee
was getting cold.

        There was
        a pause that
        permeated
        the glance
    that they
    shared
    as they
    ate more

            politely
            than
            strangers
            do in a

            café.

There were words
that needed
to be
said.

Those
quiet words
of a quiet man
who fell too quickly.

He had fallen too quickly.

120

"I love you, Sam!"

He created a line with a word.

And he knew it.

"I hurt people..."

Sam responded without his smile.

There was a distinction
neither expected to find

here.

"You haven't hurt me, Sam."

A hopeful isolation
of the message
being sent.

"You just don't know
how I've hurt you yet."

An arms race had
been started.

And the world
became cold.

And far more
sterile.

121

"I'm not sure I understand!"

Words that weren't often
spoken within the walls
of this apartment.

"I'm not sure I understand you, Sam!"

He couldn't help but seem begging
the question in his glance
of tamed defiance.

"Can we talk about this?"

He diminished the phrases into
commands with improper inflection.

Little seemed to be reasonable
in the moment and he hated it.

122

"I'm not sure, Michael!"

A
rare
comment
      from
      Sam.

      But this
      moment
            was
            rare.

"I think I better go."

      Too many
      distinctions
            had
            been
            made.

They no longer romanticized the other.

      Each other.

      Or their
      selves.

"I have things to do."

He
was
reminded
of
the
hell
in
Sam's
touch.

And
the
withdrawal
of
heaven.

"I'll call you."

123

Sam walked across
the uneven
kitchen floor.

To the door
that was now
becoming a
stranger.

The world
within the
other was
lifting with
each step.

He felt as
though he
was passing
a kidney stone.

"You don't have to leave,
Sam!"

He said in words
that couldn't be
more condemned.

Sam became a stranger.

124

Sam closed the door
  behind him.

Casually and
without spirit.

He sat on
the couch.

The cotton
still on the
white road.

Cold coffee still on the table.

The vagueness
of the world
of things
became
clear.

"These things happen..."

Whispered in the hinge

of the closing door.

Michael simply sat in the apartment

and allowed the day to come.

Sam's continual return ceased

with a final good-bye.

"Perhaps."

125

They were lost

      in
      search

         of
         illumination.

            Wandering

               the
               world

        within

  the
  other

            the vertical lines
            of walking light

        surrounded
        them.

     As they had
     fought in
     darkness,

they lost their glory.

And they were

defeated.

. . .

www.ingramcontent.com/pod-product-compliance
Lightning Source LLC
Chambersburg PA
CBHW030649260626
47157CB00007B/2568